The Clumsies make a mess of the Seaside

First published in paperback in Great Britain by HarperCollins *Children's Books* 2010
HarperCollins *Children's Books* is a division of HarperCollins*Publishers* Ltd
77-85 Fulham Palace Road, Hammersmith, London W6 8JB

Visit us on the web at www.harpercollins.co.uk

5

ISBN: 978-0-00-733935-8

The Clumsies

make a mess
of the
Seaside

By
Sorrel
Anderson
Klumsiez

Illustrated by
Nicola Slater

HarperCollins Children's Books

For David (BWFR!)

Contents

It was a Tuesday morning and the Clumsies were sitting around in Howard's office eating breakfast.

'I've been thinking,' said Purvis, sipping his tea.

'*Mmm,*' said Mickey Thompson, with a mouth full of toast.

'Could I have some more toast?'

Purvis put some bread in the toaster.

'I said I've been thinking.'

'Could I have some more juice?' asked Mickey Thompson.

Purvis passed him the juice.

'I said I've been…'

'Could I have… um… an

enormous

cake?' asked Mickey Thompson.

'And a badger.'

There was a small scuffle.

'Go on then,' said Mickey Thompson, once they'd finished. 'Tell us what you've been thinking.'

Purvis poured himself another cup of tea.

'Well,' he said. 'I'm worried about Howard.'

'Why?' asked Mickey Thompson, buttering cheerfully.

'He's working too hard,' said Purvis, 'and he seems to be in a bit of a...'

'Mood,' said Mickey Thompson.

'No,' said Purvis, 'in a bit of a...'

'Mess,' said Mickey Thompson.

'Err...' said Purvis, 'in a bit of a—'

Suddenly the door

crashed

open and Howard rushed in, ran around in a circle and rushed

out again. 'Rush?' said Mickey Thompson.

'Exactly,' said Purvis. 'He needs a holiday. I've been doing loads of research: here!'

He cleared a space and plunked
down an old-looking book titled
The Wise Traveller; a young-looking
book called *Flossy Has Fun at the
Sea*; a brochure headed *European
River Cruising*; and a leaflet

advertising
Undiscovered Essex.

Mickey
Thompson
picked up the
brochure and
studied it.

'Doesn't it
look lovely?' said Purvis, 'I–'

The door
crashed
open again and Howard rushed
back in.

'*QUICK!*' Howard shouted,

opening

cupboards

and

drawers.

'Tea?' offered Mickey Thompson.

'NO!'

'Sausage?' offered Purvis.

'*NO!*' shouted Howard, shutting drawers and cupboards. '*I haven't got time for breakfast.*'

Ortrud the elephant **TRUMPETED** in alarm.

'No time for breakfast?' said Mickey Thompson, sounding shocked.

'*I'M LATE!*' shouted Howard, running about.

'But Howard,' said Purvis.

'You're the same time as you usually are.'

Howard stopped running.

'I know, but today I needed to be early. The trouble is, I can't remember why.'

He sat down with a sigh and the Clumsies dived under the desk.

'*WHAT?*' shouted Howard, leaping up.

'There's someone coming,' whispered Purvis. The door **crashed** open and in came Mr Bullerton, Howard's boss.

'You! Howard Armitage!' barked Mr Bullerton. **'You're late. Where've you been?'**

'Err, I—' began Howard.

'Be quiet,' snapped Mr Bullerton.

'Sorry, I—'

'And stop interrupting,' said Mr Bullerton. 'Are you ready?'

'Well—' said Howard.

'You don't look anywhere *near* ready,' said Mr Bullerton. 'It starts at one you know. We must catch the eleven o'clock train or we won't get there on time.'

'There?' asked Howard.

Mr Bullerton stared at Howard.

'You can't have forgotten. Don't tell me you've *forgotten*.'

'No,' said Howard.

'You *have*, haven't you?'

'Yes,' said Howard.

Mr Bullerton went very red and stuck his face very close to Howard's ear.

'CONFERENCE!' he shouted.

'Wupf!' said Howard, jumping.

'CONFERENCE! CONFERENCE! CON. FER. RENCE!'

'Oh yes,' said Howard. 'Oh dear.'

'How dare you oh dear?' said Mr Bullerton.

'It isn't oh dear: it's a Very Important event. In a Very Important place.'

'Yes of course,' said Howard, 'I—'

'And,' continued Mr Bullerton, 'it's Very, Very Important that it goes extremely well. A lot of Very Important people are going to be there.'

'Oh?' said Howard. 'Who?'

'ME,' said Mr Bullerton, 'and I'll be watching you, Howard

Armitage, so you'd better make
sure you don't mess anything up
this time.'

'I'll try not to,' said Howard.

'You will if you know what's
good for you,' said Mr Bullerton.

'The only thing is…' said
Howard.

Mr Bullerton made a
growling noise in his
throat.

'The only thing is, I haven't
made any arrangements for my
dog. I'll have to get him, and bring
him.'

'You most certainly won't,' said Mr Bullerton.

'But I can't leave Allen at home alone all night,' said Howard. 'I'm sure the organisers would understand.'

'*I* am the organiser,' said Mr Bullerton, 'and I say *no dogs are allowed. Especially not yours.*' He **stomped** out of the room and ***slammed*** the door.

Howard sat down with a **groan** and the Clumsies came out from under the desk.

'What's going on, Howard?' asked Purvis. 'What's a conference?'

'It's a kind of large meeting,' said Howard, 'in a smart hotel by the sea. We're supposed to go there by train this morning and stay overnight.'

Purvis and Mickey Thompson started **squeaking** and jumping about.

'Now what?' said Howard.

'HURRAY!' shouted Purvis.
'WE'RE GOING ON HOLIDAY!'

'No,' began Howard, 'it isn't a—'

'WE'RE GOING TO

THE SEASIDE!' shouted
Mickey Thompson.

'No, not y–' began Howard.

'Oh I can't wait, I can't wait,'
said Mickey Thompson. 'I've never
been on holiday before.'

'Quick, we'd better start
packing,' said Purvis, rummaging.

'It's just what you need,
Howard. Look!' He handed
Howard *Flossy Has Fun at the Sea*.

'Delightful,' said Howard, 'but
listen, I'm afraid you can't c–'

'Howard,' said Purvis, 'hadn't
you better go and get Allen? We

don't want to miss the train.'

'Well yes but how can I?' said Howard. 'You heard what Mr Bullerton said.'

The mice gazed up at Howard, and Howard gazed down at the mice.

'We can't go on holiday without Allen,' said Purvis.

'We can't leave Allen behind,' said Mickey Thompson.

'No,' sighed Howard. 'You're right. Of course we can't.'

*

So the Clumsies began to pack and Howard set off to collect Allen. He walked up the long corridor to the lift and was just about to press the button when there was a

booming

voice behind him.

'Hoy,' said Mr Bullerton, advancing.

'Quick,' said Howard, pressing.

'YOU!' said Mr Bullerton, approaching.

'QUICK!' said Howard, **j-a-b-b-i-n-g**.

'STOP!' said Mr Bullerton, arriving.

'PING!' went the lift doors, opening and Howard rushed inside.

'PING! PING! PING!' went the lift doors closing and opening and closing again as Mr Bullerton grabbed hold of Howard and pulled him out.

'And where do you think you're going?' said Mr Bullerton.

'Well,' said Howard, 'I forgot to bring my overnight things, so I

thought I'd better just pop home
and—'

'Oh no you don't,' said Mr
Bullerton. 'You'll pop nowhere.'

'But—' began Howard.

'No **popping**,' said Mr
Bullerton. '**AND NO DOGS**.
Get back to your office.'

Howard got back to his office.

'That was quick,' said Purvis.

'I haven't been anywhere yet,'
said Howard. 'Mr Bullerton's
lurking. He won't let me leave.
And what's all this… everything…
everywhere?'

'The packing,' said
Purvis.

'There's too much,' said
Howard.

'We haven't finished yet,' said Mickey Thompson.

'Yes,' said Howard, 'that's what I'm worried about.'

'It'll be better soon,' said Purvis.

'Why don't you climb out of the window, Howard?'

'I beg your pardon?' said Howard.

'To avoid Mr Bullerton,' explained Purvis.

'We're on the fifth floor,' said Howard.

'Well let's see,' said Purvis, peering. 'There might be a ladder or something.'

'We're on the fifth floor,' said Howard.

'There,' said Purvis, pointing. 'You can climb down that scaffolding.'

'Oh thank you,' said Howard. 'So very much.'

'Eek,' said Mickey Thompson. 'It makes me feel DIZZY just looking at it.'

'You and me both,' said Howard. 'I think I'll try the normal way once more, if you don't mind.' He opened the door a crack, peeped out and shut it again, quickly.

'Still lurking?' asked Purvis.

'Still lurking,' said Howard.

'Why don't we ring your house
and ask Allen to come here?'
suggested Mickey Thompson.

'Because he's a dog,' said
Howard. 'He doesn't know how to
use a phone.'

'I'll bet he does,' said Mickey
Thompson. 'You didn't know he
could talk until we told you.'

'Maybe so,' said Howard, 'but
I only have your word for that
and—'

The mice started **squeaking**, indignantly.

'And anyway,' continued Howard, 'there are a lot of busy roads between there and here and I don't want him crossing them alone. Somehow, I'm going to have to go and fetch him. Somebody put the kettle on so we can think.'

So Purvis put the kettle on and they thought.

'Maybe you could speak to Mr Bullerton and persuade him,' said Purvis. 'Make him think a dog would be a good idea.'

'No,' said Howard. 'He won't and it isn't. He needs distracting, not persuading.'

'Maybe we could hypnotise him,' suggested Mickey Thompson.

'*Ridiculous,*' said Howard.

'…Or…or…lull him to sleep with a song.'

'Mickey Thompson,' said Howard, 'if I go up to Mr Bullerton and start singing lullabies at him, he'll think I've gone completely mad.'

'He already thinks that,' said Mickey Thompson, cheerfully.

'Harrumph,' said Howard. 'Come along. Sensible suggestions, please.'

'Oo!' said Purvis, hopping. 'This is what we do: we lure him to his room. We **slam** the door. We **jam** it shut and keep him in there: **TRAPPED**!'

'I know the feeling,' muttered

Howard. 'Hmm, not bad but I'm
not sure about the luring bit. Had
you anything in mind?'

'I hadn't got that far,' said
Purvis.

'We could leave a trail of cake,' said

Mickey Thompson.

'It wouldn't work,' said Howard.
'Mr Bullerton doesn't like cake.'

'Biscuits then,' said Mickey Thompson.

'Or bits of bread, even.'

'No, no,' said Howard. 'No.'

'How about this?' said Purvis.
'We ring his phone. He goes to his room to answer it. You keep him talking Howard and w—'

'What!' said Howard.

'What what?' said Purvis.

'What am I supposed to talk to him about?'

'Oh you know,' said Purvis. 'Just some sort of general chitchat.'

'Fabulous,' said Howard, 'and how…oh never mind. I expect I'll think of something. Well go on, go on.'

'Right,' said Purvis, 'so it's rings, room, answers, talking then we shut him in there: **BANG!** And then you go and get Allen,' he added. 'Howard?'

'He's gone to sleep,' said Mickey Thompson, poking.

'Stop that,' said Howard. 'I am not asleep; I'm attempting to block things out.'

'So what do you think?' said Purvis.

'It won't work,' said Howard.

'But it's for Allen, Howard,' said Purvis.

'Woof,' said Mickey Thompson, plaintively. *'Woof.'*

'Yes, yes, all right,' sighed Howard. 'I suppose it's worth a try.'

So Howard dialled Mr Bullerton's number and Purvis peeped out into the corridor.

'It's ringing,' said Howard.

'He's moving,' said Purvis. 'Let's go.'

The mice climbed on to Ortrud

and rode up the corridor to Mr Bullerton's room. They arrived just as he was answering the phone.

'Bullerton,' said Mr Bullerton.

'Hhgrr,' said Howard.

'Who is this?'

said Mr Bullerton, crossly.

'Err,' said Howard.

'Howard Armitage,' said Mr Bullerton. 'Well? What do you want?'

'Ah,' said Howard.

'What?' said Mr Bullerton.

'I was wondering…' said Howard.

'What?' said Mr Bullerton.

'Something,' said Howard. 'I was wondering… something… but now… I've forgotten.'

'I shall hang up in a minute,' said Mr Bullerton.

'Hmm,' said Howard. 'Mm?'

'I'm hanging up,' said Mr Bullerton and **slammed** the receiver down just as his office door **slammed** shut.

'*Got him!*' said Mickey Thompson.

'Lost him,' said Purvis as the office door slammed open and Mr Bullerton **shot** out, tripped over Ortrud and rolled across the corridor straight into the lift.

'**TOOT!**' went Ortrud, trumpeting.

Howard Forgets

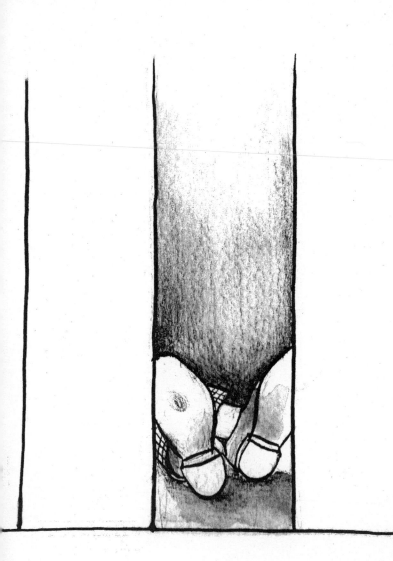

'**PING!**' went the lift doors, closing.

'LET ME OUT!' yelled Mr Bullerton, *thumping*.

'Oo-err,' said the lift.

'**THUMP,**' went Mr Bullerton.

'Well really,' said the lift.

'Are you all right?' asked Purvis.

'It's a bit much, isn't it?' said the lift.

'I know,' agreed Purvis.

The lift gave a small cough. 'And

the trouble now, you see…'

'What is it?' asked Purvis.

'I don't like to mention it, but…'

'Go on,' said Purvis.

'The thing is,' whispered the lift, 'something seems to be stuck.'

'Are you sure?' whispered Purvis.

'THUMP,' went Mr Bullerton.

'THUMP.'

'Very,' said the lift.

Purvis and Mickey Thompson exchanged glances.

'Listen,' whispered Purvis, 'we'll get you some help as quickly as we can but…'

'**THUMP**THUMP **THUMP**,' went Mr Bullerton.

'Take as long as you need,' said the lift. 'Tell you what – I think I might *whoosh* up and down a bit while I'm waiting. It'll help to pass the time.'

'*WHOOOSH!*'

went the lift, *whooshing* off.

'**WHAAAAH!**' went

Mr Bullerton, *whooshing* off too.

The Clumsies hurried back to
Howard's office, where Howard
was waiting.

'Err, Howard,' said Purvis.

'What have you done?' said
Howard.

'It wasn't us,' said Mickey
Thompson. 'It was the lift.'

'What was the lift?' said
Howard.

'It was the lift that trapped him, and stuck him,' explained Purvis.

'And now it's *whooshing* him up and down,' added Mickey Thompson.

'So you can go and get Allen now,' said Purvis. 'Howard?'

'He's dozed off again,' said Mickey Thompson.

'NO!' shouted Howard, springing up and running about. 'YES! NO! YES! RIGHT! QUICK! I'll fetch Allen. You find the lift oil.'

'Lift oil?' said Purvis.

'Well we can't leave him in there, can we? LET'S GET GOING!'

Twenty minutes later they met back at the lift, which was still *whooshing.*

'Where's Allen?' said Purvis.

'WHEEEE!' giggled the lift.

'Waiting under the desk,' said Howard.

'Help,' moaned Mr Bullerton.

'MR BULLERTON?' shouted Howard.

'ARMITAGE?' shouted Mr

Bullerton. **'GET ME OUT OF THIS THING THIS INSTANT!!!'**

'HOLD ON,' shouted Howard. **'WE'LL HAVE YOU OUT IN A JIFFY.'**

'NOW!!!!' bellowed Mr Bullerton.

'Where's that lift oil, quick,' said Howard.

'Here,' said Purvis, and he handed over a large jar with the words 'LIFT OYL' written on it, and something slimy in it.

Howard opened the lid, sniffed,

and closed it again fast.

'Oo-err,' said the lift.

'What is this?' choked Howard.

'Well we couldn't find any lift oil as such,' explained Purvis, 'so we improvised.'

'WHOOSH!' went the lift.
'THUMP,' went Mr Bullerton. 'NOW!!!! GET ME OUT NOW!!!!'

'**COMING!**' shouted Howard.

'Hang on – what'll I do with it?'

'Smear it?' suggested Mickey Thompson.

'No, fling it,' said Purvis.

'Oo I say,' said the lift. 'Do you know, I–'

Howard took off the lid, took aim, and **flung.**

'**PING!**' went the lift doors opening as the Lift Oyl

flew through the air.

'EUGH!' went Mr Bullerton, spluttering, as the Lift Oyl hit him in the face.

'Mr Bullerton!' said Howard.

'I shall see you on the train,' said Mr Bullerton, **sliding** out of the lift.

'Yes, Mr Bullerton,' said Howard.

'I am going for a bath,' said Mr Bullerton,

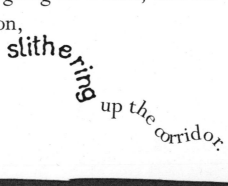

slithering up the corridor.

'Yes, Mr Bullerton,' said Howard.
'AND NOW GET
OUT OF MY
SIGHT!!!' roared Mr
Bullerton.

'Right away, Mr Bullerton,' said
Howard.

Howard led the mice and Allen and Ortrud into the station.

'Right,' he said, 'this way. Platform Eight'

'Hang on,' said Purvis, checking his notebook.

'What is it?' said Howard.

'*When undertaking a journey of any length, the wise traveller goes well-equipped with provisions to stave off hunger, or boredom,*' read out Purvis.

'*Armed with a basket of home-made sweetmeats and the latest murder-mystery, or romance, one can face with equanimity any eventuality, disruption or delay.*'

'What?' said Howard.

'It means we should take things to **eat** and **read**,' Purvis explained.

'Especially **eat**,' said Mickey Thompson.

'Yes, yes,' said Howard, 'but there isn't time. The train leaves in ten minutes.'

'I'm feeling a little faint,' said Mickey Thompson, staggering slightly.

'Oh all right,' sighed Howard. 'Quickly, then.'

Nearby was a small kiosk selling

sweets and newspapers, so every-

one **bundled**

over.

Ortrud chose a
carton of apple
juice and a wildlife
photography
magazine.

Purvis chose a

raspberry
flapjack and the
*Extended
National Railway
Timetable.*

Mickey Thompson
picked up a packet
of sherbet
fizz-bombs and a
comic called
Kerr-Blamm!!!

'Let me look,'
said Howard, flicking through
Kerr-Blamm!!! 'I'm not sure it's
suitable.'

The kiosk owner gave Howard a
funny look.

'Bit young for you, isn't it,
mate?'

'It is not for me,' said Howard,

trying to sound dignified. 'It's for
… oh, never mind.'

He grabbed
a newspaper
and a packet of
mints.

'Right,' he said, 'come along,
come along.'

But Allen was dithering in the
gardening magazines' section.

'I can't decide between *Gardens
and Lawns* and *Happy Gardening*,' he
said.

'How about that one, Allen,'
suggested Purvis, pointing.

'Oo thank you, yes,' said Allen. 'He'd like this one,' said Purvis, handing it to Howard. 'Look – it's got a free packet of seeds on the front!'

'Marvellous,' said Howard, bustling everyone over to the till and paying. 'Now can we get a move-on, per-lease.'

'Allen hasn't got any sweets,' said Mickey Thompson. 'Or did you want to eat the seeds, Allen.'

'Um no,' said Allen, worriedly, 'I'd wanted to plant them, really.'

'We'll get him something on the

train,' said Howard, starting to
run.

Everyone raced after Howard
and they all arrived at platform 8
just as the train was pulling away.

'Off it goes,' said Mickey
Thompson, cheerfully.

'NOOooO!' groaned Howard, clutching his head and hopping about. 'This is all I need. I'm for it now.'

'Don't worry, Howard,' said Purvis, brandishing his book of extended timetables.

'We've got this.' He sat down and studied it, running his finger up and down the columns of tiny numbers.

'Quick,' said Howard.

'Hmm,' said Purvis. 'Well.'

'Well?' said Howard. 'What?'

'The next train to Scrumley-on-Sea is in two hours.'

'That's too late,' said Howard.

'But wait,' said Purvis, turning to a different page and running his finger along another row of numbers.

'Yes,' he said. 'I see.'

'What do you see?' said Howard. 'What? What?'

'There's a train to Pimnster via Cluckermold.'

'What good is that?' squawked Howard, bouncing. 'I don't want to go to either of those places.'

'I know,' said Purvis, 'but the Scrumley-on-Sea train also goes via Cluckermold. According to the timetable, the Pimnster train calls at Cluckermold at 11.54 and the Scrumley-on-Sea train calls at

Cluckermold at 11.55, so if we get on the Pimnster train and then get off it again at Cluckermold we should be just in time to get on to the train we were supposed to be on in the first place.' He looked up, triumphantly.

'**Brilliant!**' said Howard. 'When does it leave?'

'In two minutes,' said Purvis, 'from platform One.'

'*QUICK!*' shouted Howard, **sprinting off.** Everyone **sprinted** after him and they all bundled on to the train just in time. It was very full.

'*Good morning,*' said a loud voice. **'*This is the 11.15 to Pimnster, calling at Bidderidge, Mimmersham, Cluckermold, Upper Cluckermold, Cluckerminster and Pimnster.*'**

'Do you mind?' said a different loud voice. 'Your bag's on my foot.'

'Sorry,' said Howard, picking it up. 'Right, come along, you lot.'

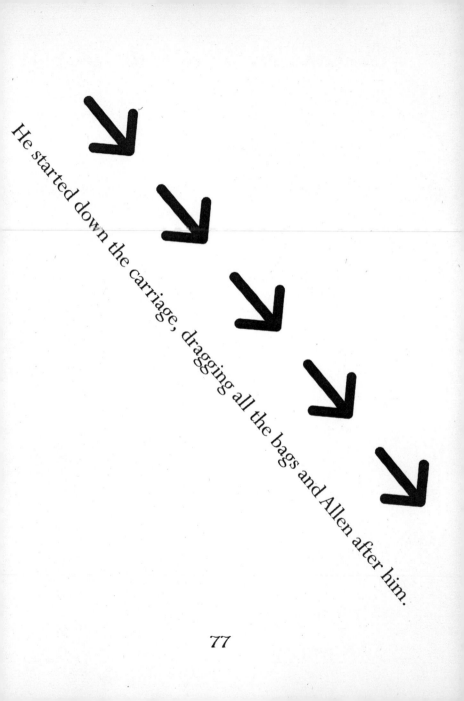

He started down the carriage, dragging all the bags and Allen after him.

Purvis and Mickey Thompson climbed on to Ortrud and followed.

'Tut,' said a woman. 'Mind my head.'

'Ouch,' said a man. 'Watch what you're doing.'

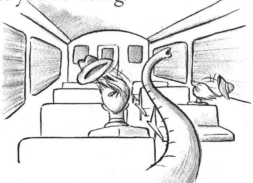

'Sorry... yes... sorry,' said Howard. But eventually they saw a spare seat in a corner by the window. Howard shoved the bags up above and Ortrud underneath and plunked down hotly, Allen on one knee and the mice on the other.

'So many people,' said Mickey Thompson. 'Pimnster must be popular.'

'Yes. Or Cluckermold,' said Purvis.

'Or Upper Clucker,' said Mickey Thompson.

Or Cluckermucker,' said Purvis, giggling.

'Or
CLICKERNICKER,'
shouted Mickey Thompson.
'CLICKERNICKERNICK
ERNICKERNICKERNIC
KERNICKER!'
Ortrud started **TRUMPETING**.
'ENOUGH!' shouted
Howard. Several of the people in
the carriage gave him funny looks.
'EXCUSE ME!' shouted
Howard. 'BIT OF A COLD!
HA HA!'
'I didn't know you had a cold,'
said Purvis.

'Shoosh,' hissed Howard. 'Let's just try and have a nice, relaxing journey, can we?' Suddenly there was a crackling, whistling noise and everyone jumped.

'HELLO LADIES AN KKCCHHHH STEW-ARD T KKCCCHHH FRASER,' said the voice, **'AND KKKCCCHHH PASTRIES, SNACKS...'**

'Listen!' said Mickey Thompson, his eyes growing rounder.

'...KKCCCHHHKKCC H WICHES, HOT BACON AND TOMATO ROLLS.'

'Where?' asked Mickey Thompson.

'I don't know, I didn't catch it,' said Howard.

'Oh,' said Mickey Thompson. 'Err, Howard?'

'Yes, Mickey Thompson,' said Howard.

'I was thinking I might go and have a little look around.'

'Mmm,' said Howard. 'I thought

you might. Don't be too long.'

So Mickey Thompson went off to find the buffet car and everyone else settled down to enjoy the journey. Ortrud went to sleep, Howard read **Kerr-Blamm!!!**, and Allen and Purvis looked out of the window.

'Howard!' said Purvis, as another train pulled alongside. 'You can see right in at everybody.'

'Mmm,' said Howard.

'*Look, Howard!*' said Purvis.

'Mmm,' said Howard, not looking.

'*It's Mr Bullerton,
Howard!*' said Purvis.

Howard dropped **Kerr-Blamm!!!**

'What? Where?'

'In that train,' said Purvis. 'I
think he's seen you: he seems to be
saying something.'

They stared out of the window
at Mr Bullerton and Mr Bullerton
glared back, mouthing.

'I can't make it out,' said Purvis.

'Oh, now he's waving.' Purvis
waved back.

'He's not waving,' said Howard,
sliding down in his seat. 'He's

shaking his fist. Come away from the window.'

'Now he's——'

Howard's mobile phone rang.

'——using his phone,' said Purvis. Howard answered it.

'Mr Bullerton!' said Howard. 'Yes, I know…yes it was but I can…no…sorry… yes…sorry, bye.'

Mr Bullerton disappeared from view as the train sped up and *swung away*.

'NEXT STATION CLUCKERMOLD,'

announced a loud voice.

'Already?' said Howard. 'What about Bidderthing and Mimmerwhateveritwas?'

'Gone,' said Purvis. 'You didn't see: you were reading Mickey Thompson's comic.'

They looked at each other.

'MICKEY THOMPSON!' shouted Howard.

'MICKEY THOMPSON!' shouted Purvis.

'I told him to be QUICK,' said

Howard, grabbing the luggage and starting to run.

'Hey!'

'Well, really,'

'Some people,'

said the people in the train as

Howard **thundered** past. Purvis, Allen and Ortrud **thundered** after him, squeaking, **woofing** and TOOTING.

They ran all the way u

the back of the train,

to the front of the train,

and all the way down to

but there was no sign of Mickey Thompson.

'CLUCKERMOLD! CLUCK-ERMOLD!' said the loud voice as they pulled into the station.

'Howard!' said Purvis, tugging at Howard's trousers and starting to panic. 'We can't get off without him, Howard!'

'Well of course not,' said Howard, 'but WHERE IS HE???'

Something prodded Purvis in the stomach. It was Mickey Thompson, with a sausage. There was a small scuffle.

'Off! Off!' said Howard,
scooping up the mice and
everyone out on to the platform
and over to a waiting train.

'On! On!' said Howard,
bustling everyone into it just in
time as the whistle blew **and
the train drew
away.**

'*Phew,*' said Purvis, once they'd found a seat and settled down again.

'Quite,' said Howard.

'Oo look,' said Mickey Thompson, pointing with the sausage at another train.

'There's Mr Bullerton!'

Everyone gazed at Mr Bullerton and Mr Bullerton gazed back as they slid slowly past in the opposite direction.

'But…' said Purvis.

'NEXT STATION MIMMERSHAM,' said a loud voice.

'Mimmersham?' said Howard. 'MIMMERSHAM??? We're on the wrong train! We're going back the way we came!'

'But we haven't been on holiday yet,' protested Mickey Thompson.

Howard's phone started ringing.

'I'll check the timetable,' said Purvis, quickly.

'I can't hear it,' said Howard. 'I won't answer it.'

'Hmm,' said Purvis. 'Now we're going in the wrong direction I'm not sure we'll get to Scrumley-on-Sea by one o'clock.'

'We absolutely **must** get to Scrumley-on-Sea by one o'clock,' said Howard.

'Don't worry,' said Purvis. 'I'll check the map: maybe there's another way round.' He rummaged in his rucksack, took out a piece of paper that was folded up very small, and unfolded it until it was very big.

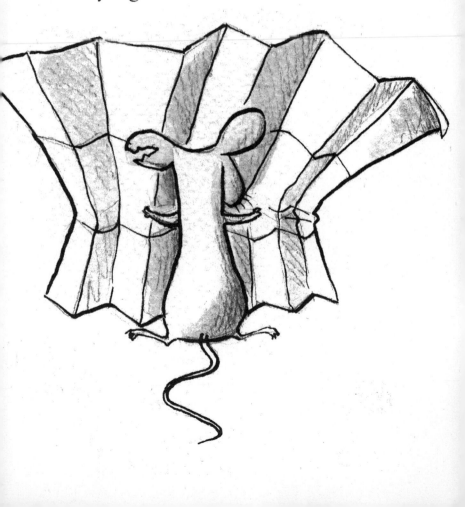

'I didn't know you had a map,'
said Howard.

'You can't go on a journey
without a map,' said Purvis. 'The
wise traveller—'

'Yes, never mind all that,' said
Howard. 'Just get on with it.'

'OK,' said Purvis.

'Well…err…if we get off at
Mimmersham I think we'll be
able to walk to a bus stop and
catch a bus that'll take us all the
way there.'

So they got off the train at
Mimmersham and began to walk.

They walked up a lane,

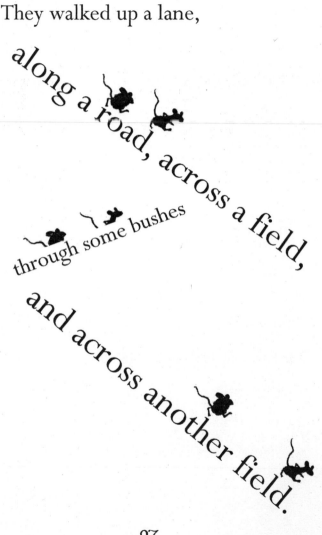

along a road, across a field,

through some bushes

and across another field.

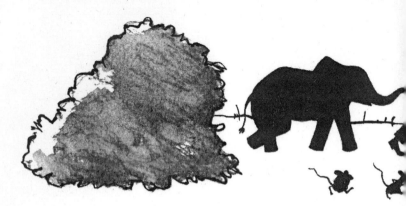

When they came to a stream Howard stopped and put down all the bags.

'Purvis,' he puffed, 'this can't be right. Let me see the map.'

Purvis passed it to Howard and Howard stared at it for what seemed like quite a long time.

'Where did you get it?' he
asked.

'I drew it, before we came,' said
Purvis. Howard sat down on the
grass and started making a
groaning noise.

'*Moo!*' said Mickey Thompson,
at Howard.

'What's the matter, Howard?'
asked Purvis, anxiously.

'You must have drawn it wrong,'
said Mickey Thompson, to Purvis.

'*MoooOOO!*'

There was a small s c *uffl*e.

'No scuffling,' said Howard,
getting up. 'It's very nicely
coloured-in, Purvis.' Purvis
beamed.

'Right,' sighed Howard. 'Come
along. We might as well keep
going. I expect we'll get somewhere
eventually.'

He led the way over to the stream

and took off his shoes and socks.

'It's very shallow. We can wade across,' he said, starting to wade across. Everyone else stood on the bank and watched.

'It doesn't look all that shallow to me,' called Mickey Thompson.

'Well climb onto Ortrud then,' called Howard.

'Ortrud can't swim,' called Mickey Thompson.

'I'm sure she can,' called Howard.

'She doesn't want to,' called Mickey Thompson.

'Climb on to Allen then.'

'Allen can't swim either,' called Purvis.

'Nonsense,' called Howard, 'dogs love to swim.'

'Allen doesn't, do you, Allen?' said Purvis.

'Well,' said Allen, 'I *can* swim, but I'm not very keen on cold water, and that stream looks *f r e e z i n g .* '

'He doesn't want to, Howard,' called Purvis.

'Carry us, Howard!' called Mickey Thompson. So Howard

took the luggage over to the other
side, then waded back and
collected Ortrud, then carried her
over to the other side, then waded
back and collected
Allen, then
carried him over to
the other side,
then waded back
and collected the
mice, then carried
them over to the other
side. Then he lay down
on the grass,
panting.

'Ah,' said Mickey Thompson.

'Ugh,' said Howard.

'Oh dear,' said Mickey Thompson.

'*What?*' said Howard.

'You've left your shoes and socks on the other side,' said Mickey Thompson. Howard waded over and back again, crossly.

But eventually they set off

over

the field
and up a hill,

and up the hill some more, and

up it even more. By the time they reached the top everyone
was very tired.

'I can't go on,' said
Howard.

'But *look*,' said Purvis.

'*There's the sea!*'

Sure enough, at the bottom of
the hill was a town and behind it
was the sea, looking *twinkley*.

'I *still* can't go on,' said Howard.
'It's *too* far, and I'm *too* tired.'

'You **must**,' said Purvis.

'Mr Bullerton will be furious if you don't turn up.'

'He's probably already furious,' said Howard.

'And you said we could have a holiday,' said Mickey Thompson. 'All we've had so far is journey and journey and *more* journey.'

'Harrumph,' said Howard.

'Hmm,' said Purvis, looking around. 'It's straight downhill from here to the hotel. If only there was some way of… **OO!**' He **raced** over to a tree and **dragged** something out from behind it. It was an old shopping trolley.

'No,' said Howard. 'Absolutely not.'

But the mice were already loading the bags and Allen and Ortrud into the trolley.

'Push, Howard,' said Purvis, climbing in.

Howard pushed.

'Get on, Howard,' said Mickey

Thompson, as they began to roll down the hill.

'I can't,' said Howard, gripping the trolley and running.

'GET ON, HOWARD!' shouted Purvis, as they clattered along faster and faster.

'HELP!' shouted Howard.

'HOWARD! GET ON!' shouted everybody.

Howard got on.

'AAAAAGGG HHHHH!!!'

they yelled as they

The Journey

shot down the hill,

crashed

through the hotel doors just as a

clock was chiming one.

'WE MADE IT!'

shouted Purvis, as the trolley

skidded across the foyer and

crashed out again,

bumping into something

solid on the way.

'WEEE-OWW!!!' wailed Mr Bullerton, as he flew through the air, and 'Umf,' he said, as he landed.

Clumsies~ On~Sea

part 1

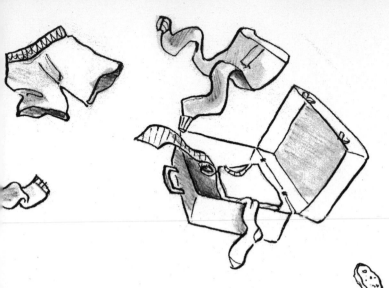

H oward climbed out of the
shopping trolley and walked back
into the hotel foyer. Mr Bullerton
was **lying** on the floor.

'Hullo, Mr Bullerton!'
said Howard, *brightly*.

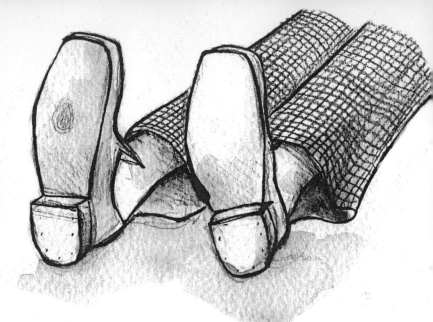

'Eh?' said Mr Bullerton.

'Let me help you up,' said Howard.

'What just happened?' said Mr Bullerton. 'Did something just happen?'

'You fell over,' said Howard.

'Where am I?' said Mr Bullerton. 'What place is this?'

'Scrumley-on-Sea,' said Howard. 'We're here on a holid—err...'

'What?' said Mr Bullerton. 'Who are *you*?'

'It's *me*,' said Howard.

'Who's...' Mr Bullerton leapt. 'YOU. I told you to be here *on time*.'

'I *am*,' said Howard.

'You *can't* be,' said Mr Bullerton. 'I saw you going the wrong way. Twice. Waving sausages.'

'No, no,' said Howard, soothingly. 'I think you must have bumped your head.'

'I'll bump your head,' said Mr Bullerton. 'Just you listen to me. I don't want any *muck-ups* with this conference. We'll have everything smooth, and everything *nice*. Yes?'

'Oh yes,' agreed Howard.

'Because,' continued Mr
Bullerton, **breathing heavily**,
'if it goes well, I'm going to get a
promotion.'

'Wonderful,' said Howard.
'Well done.'

'And if it doesn't go well, you're
going to get **fired**. *Understand?*'

'Absolutely,' said Howard.

'Good,' said Mr Bullerton. He

stomped off, so Howard
collected his room key and then
collected the Clumsies,
who were waiting
outside.

'Where's the trolley?' asked
Howard.

'We've hidden it,' said
Purvis. 'So as not to
attract attention.'

'And in case we need to make a **QUICK GETAWAY**,' said Mickey Thompson.

'Very wise,' said Howard. 'Come on then: let's go and find our room.' He picked up the bags and led the way back into the hotel.

'EXCUSE ME, SIR,'

said a **loud** voice, and everyone jumped. It was the hotel receptionist.

'Is that your dog? You can't bring a dog in here. Not unless it's a guide dog. *Is* it a guide dog?'

'No,' said Howard, 'but—'

'Well you can't bring it in then,' said the receptionist, firmly. 'You'll have to tether it in the outhouse.'

The mice gasped, and Allen gave a gulp.

'Surely not?' said Howard.

'I've said,' said the receptionist, even more firmly.

Howard led the way back out of the hotel.

'I'm ever so sorry,' said Allen.

'It isn't your fault, Allen,' said Purvis.

'Why do they not allow dogs, but don't mind about *elephants*?' asked Mickey Thompson.

'No idea,' said Howard.

'Shall we disguise Allen as an elephant?' asked Mickey Thompson.

'No,' said Howard.

'There's nothing to use,' said Purvis, looking around. 'Unless…'

He looked at Howard's suitcase.

'No,' said Howard.

'But if he was wearing clothes, they might think he's a person.'

'Unlikely,' said Howard.

'Let's try,' said Purvis.

So the mice emptied the suitcase out on to the ground and rummaged through.

'These are the right kind of length,' said Purvis, holding up a pair of boxer shorts.

'Actually,' began Howard, 'I don't really—'

125

'Try them, Allen,' said Purvis.

Allen tried them.

'And this,' said Mickey

Thompson, passing a shirt.

Allen put it on.

'I'm not sure about the colour,'

said Allen.

'Why's that?' asked

Purvis.

'What?' said Howard.

'Why's what?'

'It's a bit gaudy,'

said Allen.

Purvis giggled. 'Yes, it is a bit.'

'What?' said Howard. 'What's he saying?'

'I quite like it,' said Mickey Thompson.

'So do I,' said Howard.

'It'll just have to do for now, Allen,' said Purvis. 'It's only for getting in with – you don't have to wear it all the time.'

'That's a very nice shirt, that is,' said Howard.

'Yes, it's lovely, Howard,' said Purvis. 'Right, what's next?'

'These,' said Mickey Thompson, handing over a hat and a pair of sunglasses. Allen put those on too.

'Perfect!' said Purvis.

'I'm extremely fond of that shirt,' said Howard.

'We're ready, Howard,' said Purvis.

'Oh come along then,' said Howard. He picked up the bags and led the way back into the hotel, put-outly.

'EXCUSE ME, SIR,'

said a **loud** voice, and everyone jumped. It was the hotel receptionist.

Everyone stood very still.

'Can I help you, sir?' asked the receptionist, staring at Allen.

'NO, THANK YOU!'

shouted Howard.

Everyone moved carefully towards the lift, where a woman was waiting.

'MORNING!' shouted Howard, at the woman.

'Morning,' said the woman, staring at Allen.

'Hello!' said Purvis, to the lift.

'Shoosh,' hissed Howard. '*Try* to seem normal.'

'You *what?*' said the woman.

'What?' said Howard. 'Not you. Ha ha!'

The woman gave Howard a funny look.

'Err, SIR?' called the receptionist.

'We'll take the stairs,' said Howard, and everyone charged over to the staircase and raced up a flight, around a corner, up another flight,

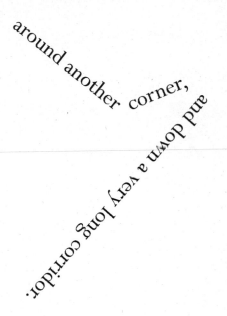

around another corner, and down a very long corridor.

'Just like being back in the office,' observed Mickey Thompson.

'Hmph,' said Howard,

stopping in front of a door. 'Here we are. 216.' He unlocked the door and they all stepped through into a large room, which had flowery-patterned walls, flowery-patterned curtains, and a bed with a flowery-patterned bedspread on it. 'Biscuits!' said Mickey Thompson, pointing. 'Tea bags,' said Howard, staggering.

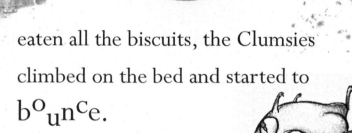

When they'd drunk all the tea and

eaten all the biscuits, the Clumsies

climbed on the bed and started to

b^ouⁿ^ce.

'Right,' said Howard.

'Whee!'

said Mickey

Thompson.

'Listen,' said Howard.

'We're listening,' said Purvis.

'I've got to go to the conference now.'

'Whe-hey!'
said Mickey Thompson.

'Will you be all right while I'm gone?'

'Of course,' said Purvis, still bouncing.

'Don't make a mess. Don't break anything.'

'We'll go and *play* on the beach,' said Purvis.

'Don't get lost, and don't do anything... **silly**.'

'Of course not,' said Purvis. 'I've got my notes: we'll know what to do.'

'*Hmm,*' said Howard.

So Howard went off to the conference and the mice and Allen and Ortrud went to the beach.

There was a **narrow, pebbly bit** and a **wide sandy bit**, and a huge stretch of sea, and an enormous amount of sky. It was *lovely*.

'What's first then?' asked Mickey Thompson.

'Paddling,' said Purvis, and they all raced down to the edge of the sea and then raced back again, squealing.

'I got **splashed!**' said Allen.

'We're supposed to stand right in, and kick about,' said Purvis.

'Let's do that later,' said Mickey Thompson. 'When it's warmer.'

'OK,' said Purvis, turning to the next page in his notebook. 'Um, Having a Donkey Ride,' he announced.

'Are you sure?' asked Mickey Thompson, sounding doubtful.

'That's what it says,' said Purvis.

'Oh look, there's one over there.'

Otrud gave a loud **TRUMPET** and started *galloping* towards the donkey. By the time the mice and Allen had caught up, Ortrud and the donkey were sharing a carrot.

'Hello!' said Purvis, to the donkey.

The donkey blinked at him, and carried on chewing.

'Can we have a ride?' asked
Mickey Thompson.

The donkey sighed, and carried
on chewing.

'Can we have a carrot?' asked
Mickey Thompson, giggling a bit.

The donkey stopped chewing
and went very still.

'This your elephant?'

'Err, yes,' said Purvis. 'Sorry if
she… your carrot… err…'

'S'all right. I quite like
elephants,' said the donkey, and
started chewing again.

'Good. Well, thank you,
Elizabeth,' said Purvis.

The donkey didn't say anything
else so they set off back down the beach.

142

Ortrud **trotted** after them.

'*Elizabeth?*' said Mickey Thompson.

'It was written on her harness thing,' said Purvis.

'She didn't seem too keen on the ride idea,' said Allen.

'It was probably her break or something,' said Purvis, turning to the next page in his notebook. 'We can try again later. Right. Um, Making a Sandcastle,' he

announced, and they set to work
digging scrabbling, and patting. Once they'd made a big mound of sand they stood back to have a look.

'Done?' asked Mickey Thompson.

'I'm not sure,' said Purvis. 'It isn't very... err...'

'Castley?' said Allen.

'Mmm,' said Purvis, 'it's a bit too...'

'Sandy?' said Mickey Thompson.

'Possibly,' said Purvis. 'It needs a little something more, somehow.'

'Shells,' said a voice, and everyone jumped. It was the

donkey, Elizabeth, with a paper
bag full of shells.

'To *decorate* the sides with,' she
explained. 'I've seen people do it,
before.'

 'Elizabeth!' said Purvis. 'They're
just what we need!'

So the mice and Allen carefully
decorated the sandcastle with
shells while Ortrud and Elizabeth
stood next to each other and
watched.

They'd just finished when a large grey cloud floated in front of the sun.

'Poor Howard,' said Purvis, **shivering.**

'What's *Howard*?' asked Elizabeth.

'Not a *what*, a *who*,' said Mickey Thompson.

'Bless you,' said Elizabeth.

'Why?' said Mickey Thompson.

'What?' said Elizabeth.

'No, not a *what*,' said Mickey Thompson. 'He's a *him*.'

'A *person*,' said Purvis.

'And why *poor*?' said Elizabeth. 'Poor why?'

'Oh,' said Mickey Thompson, **'Mr Bullerton.'** He made a face and gesticulated.

'Howard's boss,' explained Purvis.

'I see,' said Elizabeth.

'And he really needed a *holiday*. He'll have missed it all by the time he gets out.'

'At least he had a little paddle in that stream,' said Mickey Thompson.

'That doesn't really count,' said Purvis.

'I wish I had a camera,' said Allen. 'Then I'd take a photo of the sandcastle, and give it to him.'

'We could do a drawing and give him that,' suggested Mickey Thompson, '... or... or... a collage, with real sand stuck on.'

'Um, err...' said Allen.

'What's up, Allen?' asked Purvis.

'I'm a little bit worried the sand'll fall off,' said Allen.

'Oh,' said Mickey Thompson, crestfallen.

'But wait,' said Purvis, hopping about. 'We could take the real,

actual, real sandcastle up to the room and give him that: all of it! Then he'll get the full effect.'

'Shall I fetch the trolley?' asked Mickey Thompson. 'We can put it in, and push it up.'

'*Err, um...*' said Allen.

'What is it, Allen?' asked Purvis.

'I'm a little bit **worried** the sand'll fall through,' said Allen.

'Oh,' said Purvis and Mickey Thompson together.

'*A-hem,*' said Elizabeth. 'Wheelbarrow. This way.'

They followed Elizabeth up the

beach and into a stableyard, where there was a large wheelbarrow.

'It's full of *stuff*,' said Mickey Thompson.

'Not any more,' said Elizabeth, tipping it.

So they trundled the barrow back to the sandcastle, took the shells off, loaded the sand in, put the shells on and trundled into the hotel, where Mr Bullerton was talking to the receptionist.

They trundled out again, quickly.

'*Whoops,*' said Mickey Thompson.

'*I've forgotten my shirt,*' wailed Allen.

'You'd better hide under the sand,' said Purvis.

'What about the little elephant?' asked Elizabeth.

'It seems to be only *dogs* they mind,' explained Mickey Thompson.

So they took everything out of

the wheelbarrow, helped Allen in
and put everything back on top of
him.

'*Comfy, Allen?*' asked Purvis.

'Gg cchh gggg,' said Allen,
muffledly.

'*What* did he say?' asked
Mickey Thompson.

'Not sure,' said Purvis.

Allen's nose appeared.

'That's better,' he said.

'Try and keep rather still, Allen,'

said Mickey Thompson, scooping
sand back into the barrow.

Purvis peeped into the hotel.

'We're in luck. They've *gone*.'

'Shall I get out then?' asked
Allen.

'Best stay in,' said Purvis, 'to be
on the safe side. Let's go *QUICK*,
before they come back.'

They trundled unsteadily
across the foyer and arrived
at the lift.

'Afternoon there, Elizabeth,' said the lift, v-e-r-y s-l-o-w-l-y.

'Afternoon there,' said Elizabeth, v-e-r-y s-l-o-w-l-y back.

'How's you then, Elizabeth?' said the lift.

'Not so bad,' said Elizabeth. 'You?'

'Terrible,' said the lift.

Purvis and Mickey Thompson exchanged glances.

'Pulley trouble, is it?' said

Elizabeth.

'Not half,' said the lift. 'They're not what they used to be, not what they used to be at all.'

'Are they not?' said Elizabeth.

'They are not,' said the lift.

'Ah well,' said Elizabeth.

'Ah well,' agreed the lift.

'Ah well,' said Elizabeth.

'Ah well,' confirmed the lift.

'Err…' said Purvis, 'do you think maybe we ought to… before someone…'

The Clumsies make a Mess of the Seaside

'Ah. Now,' said the lift. 'What're you doing with all this lot here then, Elizabeth?'

'Just helping out with a little job,' said Elizabeth.

'Oh-ah,' said the lift. 'Where to, then?'

'Sec–' began Purvis.

'Where'll it be?' said the lift.

'Sec–' began Purvis.

'Oo,' said the lift, 'I know how you feel, lovey. I suffer with *hiccups* myself. I do, don't I, Elizabeth?'

'You do,' said Elizabeth.

'Not *half* I do.'

The lift lapsed into silence.................................

....

....

....

....

Clumsies~On~Sea (Part 1)

....

....

....

....

....

....

....

....

....

....

....

....

....

....

....

....

....

....

'*Err...*' said Purvis.

'*Ah,*' said the lift. 'Now. Wanting

to go somewhere, were you?'

'Second floor. Please,' said

Purvis.

'Right you are. Should've said,' said the lift

and **clunked** them – slowly – up to the second floor.

But when they got to the room the door wouldn't open.

'That's funny,' said Purvis. 'Howard said he'd leave it unlocked for us.'

'No problem,' said Elizabeth. 'Stand back.'

They stood back, and Elizabeth **bashed** the door open with her bottom.

'**TRUMPET!**' went Ortrud.

'YELP!' went Allen.

'KER-RASH!!!' said Mickey Thompson.

'Oh dear,' said Purvis.

'S'all yours,' said Elizabeth. 'Now you can give him something to knock his socks off.'

Clumsies On-Sea
part 2

The Clumsies and Elizabeth
pushed the wheelbarrow into the
room and tipped the shells and the
sand and Allen out on to the floor.

'Um…' said Allen.

'Right,' said Purvis. 'What we need to do is make the sandcastle look as good as we possibly can. Then the door won't seem so…'

'Err…' said Allen.

'Unusual?' said Mickey Thompson.

'Noticeable,' said Purvis.

'I'm feeling a little bit *sick*,' said Allen. 'It was bumpy in the barrow.'

'You need a biscuit, Allen,'

said Mickey Thompson, pointing at
the biscuit basket.

'Look, we've got
new ones.'

'Yes, please,' said
Allen.

'Allen needs a
biscuit before we start, Purvis,'
said Mickey
Thompson.

'OK,' said Purvis.

'I expect Ortrud would like one

too,' said Mickey Thompson.

Ortrud **TOOTED**.

'OK,' said Purvis.

'Err, Purvis,' said Mickey Thompson.

'Ok,' said Purvis.

'I'll put the kettle on.'

Once they'd
drunk all
the tea

and eaten all the biscuits everyone

set to work ass em bling

Howard's sandcastle.

They **patted** the sand

into shape and stuck on the shells,

and when they'd finished they

stood back to have a look.

'It looks *beautiful*,' said Allen.

'Hmm,' said Purvis, sounding uncertain.

'It looks **enormous**,' said Mickey Thompson.

'Hmm,' said Purvis, sounding worried.

'It looks really strange having a sandcastle sticking up from the middle of the carpet like that,' said Elizabeth.

'Yes,' said Purvis, 'it does. I think we need to make it blend in a bit.'

'We could paint the carpet yellow, to match the sand,' suggested Mickey Thompson.

'I'd say the sand's more a lightish brown kind of a colour really,' said Allen.

'And we haven't got any paint,' said Purvis.

'Custard, then,' said Mickey Thompson.

'Eh?' said everyone.

'There's probably loads of custard in this hotel. If we get some and pour it over the carpet, the sandcastle won't stand out so much.'

'In a way,' said Purvis.

'But it would still be a little too yellow, I think,' said Allen.

'*Mustard* then,' said Mickey Thompson. 'Mustardy Custard. CUSTARDY—'

'*Shhhhh!*' said Purvis. 'We want it to look like a *beautiful* beach, not a load of *spilt dinner.*'

There was a small scuffle.

'Stop!' said Elizabeth. They stopped.

'Save it for later,' said Elizabeth.

'Let's just get some extra sand and sprinkle it.'

'Off we go again then,' said Mickey Thompson, *cheerfully*, and headed for the door.

'Err…' said Allen.

'What is it, Allen?' said Purvis.

'I was wondering,' said Allen,

looking around.

'Yes, Allen?' said Purvis.

'Maybe I should stay here and guard the sandcastle. I just thought it might be a good idea.'

'It is! Thanks, Allen,' said Purvis.

'We wouldn't want anything to happen to it, would we?' said Allen.

'You're quite right, Allen,' said Purvis.

'It's probably best if I do

it from up here, actually,' said
Allen, jumping on to the bed. 'I'll
get a better view that way.'

'Good plan,' said Purvis. 'See
you soon, Allen.'

There was no reply.

'We won't be long,'
said Purvis.

There was a loud

snore

from the bed, so the others set off:
back-along-the-corridor-and-into-

the-lift-and-out-of-the-lift-and-
through-the-empty-foyer-and-all-
the-way-down-to-the-beach,-and-
filled-the barrow-with-sand,-and-
turned-to-trundle-back-again.

'Wait!' said Elizabeth.

They waited.

'More shells,' said Elizabeth.

They added more shells.

'And seaweed,' directed Elizabeth. So they gathered some seaweed.

'Also pebbles,' said Elizabeth, and they trotted off to find some pebbles.

'Look at this,' called Mickey Thompson, k i c k i n g a large flat one.

'Oh!' said the pebble. Mickey Thompson fell over backwards.

'That isn't a *pebble*,' said Purvis, prodding. 'It's a crab.'

'Oh, oh,' said the crab. 'Stop that. Stop it.'

'Oo, sorry,' said Purvis.

'I'm **bruised**,' said the crab.
'You've **bruised** me all over.'

'I'm *really* sorry,' said Purvis,
'we didn't—'

'Great rough j-a-b-b-i-n-g
fingers. Why must you use me so
harshly? Mm? Mmmm?'

'Oh dear…' said Purvis.

'Oh look!' said Mickey
Thompson. 'Here comes
Elizabeth! *Help*, Elizabeth.'

Elizabeth arrived and peered down at the crab.

'Allright, Lenny?'

'Leonard,' tutted the crab.

'Good afternoon, Elizabeth and thank you for your *kind* enquiry but no I am *not* allright. I am very much *not* allright *indeed.*'

Purvis and Mickey Thompson exchanged glances.

'Why's that then, Len?' said Elizabeth.

'Leonard,' said the crab.

'Because I'm covered in bruises, that's why.'

'You'll live,' said Elizabeth. 'Coming along with us then, Lenny-boy? Fancy a little outing? Might *cheer* you up.'

'*Leonard*,' said the crab, 'and no I do not. I do *not* need *cheering* up: I'm perfectly fine.'

'That's the spirit,' said Elizabeth.

'Apart from the bruises,' said

Leonard, quickly. 'So, err… where are you going, anyway?'

'Hotel,' said Elizabeth, nodding in that direction.

'You must be *mad*,' said Leonard. 'How can I be expected to undertake such a trip in my condition? *Mm? Mmmm?*'

'Later then, Len,' said Elizabeth, starting to walk away.

'Wait,' said Leonard. 'Oh allright, I'll come. I suppose.'

'Hotel it is,' said Elizabeth, so they plunked Leonard on top of the wheelbarrow and trundled back to the hotel.

'Oh ow,' said Leonard. 'Mind, will you? You're bumping me.'

'Sorry, Lenny-boy,' said Mickey Thompson, brightly.

'*Shoosh*,' giggled Purvis.

'What's all the *shooshing*?'

snapped Leonard, as they rushed through the empty foyer and arrived at the lift.

'All go today, Elizabeth,' said the lift, v - e - r - y s - l - o - w - l - y .

'S'all go today,' agreed Elizabeth, v - e - r - y s - l - o - w - l - y back.

'Got Nev helping out too, have you?' said the lift, looking at Leonard.

'What?' said Leonard.

'He fancied a little outing,' said Elizabeth.

'Oh-ah,' said the lift. 'How's you then, Nev?'

'It's *Leonard,*' said Leonard. 'El. En. Ud.'

'Right you are, lovey,' said the lift, and c^lu_nk^ed them
s - l - o - w - l - y ^up to the second floor.

'*Look*, Leonard!' said Purvis, when they arrived at the room. 'What do you think of the sandcastle?'

'Whatever on earth has happened to this *door*?' said Leonard.

'Oh… *err*…' said Purvis.

'Spot of bother,' said Elizabeth. 'I sorted it.'

'And why is there all this other mess?' said Leonard.

'Oh dear,' said Purvis.

'It isn't mess,' said Mickey Thompson. 'It's a *present*, for Howard.'

'*Poor Howard*,' said Leonard.

'That's the one,' said Elizabeth.

'Anyway,' said Purvis, quickly,

'we haven't even finished yet.

We've still got all this extra stuff

to sprinkle.'

So Purvis and Mickey Thompson

sprinkled

sand and shells and pebbles and

seaweed over and around the room

while the others watched and Allen **snored**.

'It must be nearly tea-time by now,' said Mickey Thompson, once they'd finished.

'Wha'?' said Allen, waking up. 'Did somebody mention tea-time?'

'At last,' said Leonard. 'I'm gasping.'

'*A-hem,*' said Elizabeth. 'Not so fast. You could do a lot more with that seaweed, in my opinion.'

'Oo,' said Allen.

'How do you mean?' asked Purvis.

'Make it more of a feature. 'S'nice bit of seaweed, that.'

'Not that nice,' muttered Leonard. Elizabeth *glowered* at him.

'S'very nice,' she said, firmly. 'We could drape it across the window,' suggested Purvis.

'Or
dangle
it from the ceiling,'
suggested Mickey Thompson.

'Or chuck it in the bin,'
suggested Leonard.

Elizabeth *glowered* harder.

'Not if you wants your tea and
your ride back to the beach,
Lenny-me-old-son.'

'Allright allright, keep your hair
on,' said Leonard,

^sC_u^t_T^l_i^N_g under Ortrud.

'I'VE GOT AN IDEA!' shouted Allen.

Everyone looked at Allen.

'Let's write "*HOWARD*" with it, on the bed!'

Everyone stared at Allen.

'Err...' said Allen.

'Now that,' said Elizabeth, 'is a Very Good Idea.'

'N–' began Leonard.

'What?' said Elizabeth.

'Nothing,' said Leonard.

So they wrote the word "*HOWARD*" with the

seaweed on the bed.

Suddenly there were **foot-steps** outside in the corridor.

'Here comes Howard,' said Purvis. 'Quick, let's hide in the bathroom and spring out as a surprise.'

Everyone bundled into the bathroom just in time as the **footsteps** stopped. Everyone held their breath as the broken door *creaked* open.

And everyone jumped as there was a **great roaring noise** and Mr Bullerton started to **shout**.

'VANDALISM!' **shouted** Mr Bullerton.

'MY ROOM'S BEEN VANDALISED!' **shouted** Mr Bullerton.

'I WANT THE HOTEL MANAGER!'

shouted Mr Bullerton.

'We've made a mistake,' whispered Purvis.

'That's why the door wouldn't open, then,' whispered Mickey Thompson, back.

'MANAGER!'

shouted Mr Bullerton.

There was the sound of running and someone arrived.

'Oo-err,' said the someone. 'Whatever on earth have you done?'

'ME?' **bellowed** Mr Bullerton. 'This was not ME! And why are YOU here? I don't need a receptionist: I need the manager.'

'The manager's a bit busy at the moment, sir,' said the receptionist.

'How dare you?' said Mr Bullerton. 'I. WANT. THE. MANAGER!'

'I think I'd better get the manager,' said the receptionist. 'MANAGER!'

'MANAGER!' **shouted** Mr Bullerton.

'MANAGER!' shouted the receptionist.

There was the sound of running and someone else arrived.

'I am the manager,' said the manager. 'What seems to be the…oh!'

'Yes,' said Mr Bullerton. 'Oh.'

'But *how* did you… *why* did you…?'

'DON'T YOU *HOW* AND *WHY* ME,' shouted Mr Bullerton.

'No, sir,' said the manager. 'I'VE *HOW'D* AND *WHY'D*

NOTHING,'

shouted Mr Bullerton.

'Err, yes, I mean no, sir,' said the manager.

'This room has been VANDALISED, as any fool can see. Now DO SOMETHING.'

'Excuse me,' said the receptionist.

'WHAT?'

barked Mr Bullerton.

'Who's *Howard*? Are *you* Howard?'

'I beg your pardon?' said Mr Bullerton, icily.

'Only that's what it says on the bed there. Look.'

They looked.

'Oh no,' whispered Purvis.

'That's torn it,' whispered Mickey Thompson, back.

'Howard Armitage,' said Mr Bullerton, very quietly.

'Who's *Howard Armitage*?' asked the receptionist.

'Howard Armitage,' said Mr Bullerton, a little less quietly. 'Do you know this Howard Armitage?' asked the manager. '**HOWARD ARMITAGE!**' **roared** Mr Bullerton, extremely loudly. '**GET HIM. BRING HIM TO ME.**' 'Now sir,' began the manager, 'if you'll just try and keep calm I'll…'

Further up the corridor a door
opened and Howard's head
appeared.

'Hello?' said Howard. 'I thought
I heard somebody calling my
name.'

'Ah!' said Mr Bullerton. 'Mr
Armitage. I wonder, Mr Armitage,
whether you'd mind just popping
along here for a moment, if you'd
be so good. There's something I
think you might be able to help me
with.'

'Yes,' said Howard. 'I–'

'**NOW!!!**' **roared**

Mr Bullerton.

There was the sound of *running*

and Howard arrived.

'Oh,' said the receptionist, 'him.

Yes I've seen him. He's the one who

tried to bring the dog in, earlier.'

'What?' said Mr Bullerton.

'Dog?' said the manager.

'No!' said Howard.

'You *did!*' said the

receptionist. 'It *was* you,

I'm *sure* it was. I said is it a guide dog cos if it is you can bring it in but if it isn't you can't and you said no it wasn't so I said then you couldn't and you went.'

'No, no,' said Howard.

'And then you came back in again and—'

'NO!' said Howard. 'Ha ha. No, no, no.'

'I see,' said Mr Bullerton.

'No dogs are allowed in this

hotel,' said the manager, to
Howard. 'Not unless they're guide
dogs.'

'I'd gathered that,' muttered
Howard.

The manager gave Howard a
NASTY look.

'If I was to find you had brought
a dog in here, sir, there would be
consequences.'

'Yes,' said Mr Bullerton, through
gritted teeth. 'There would.'

'Well I don't have one on me at the moment,' said Howard, 'and you're welcome to search my room. There's definitely no dog in there.'

'Don't worry, we will,' said Mr Bullerton. 'But first: *this*!' and with a **flourish** he stepped away from the door. Howard peered in.

'Oh.'

'Yes!' said Mr Bullerton, triumphantly. 'Oh! And would you

kindly explain to me why there's the word "*HOWARD*", written in seaweed, ON MY BED.'

'*Hmm,*' said Howard. 'Do you think that says "*HOWARD*"? It doesn't look like "*HOWARD*" to me; it looks more like… *err…*'

'More like *err…*?' said Mr Bullerton.

'More like, err…'

'"*HOWARD*",' **shouted** Mr Bullerton. 'IT LOOKS

MORE LIKE EXACTLY LIKE "HOWARD".'

'That doesn't necessarily mean I did it,' said Howard.

'He's got a point there,' said the receptionist.

'We need to conduct a thorough investigation of the room,' said the manager. 'There will be evidence.'

'They'll find us!' whispered Purvis.

'We're for it!' whispered Mickey Thompson, back.

'Leave it to me,' said Elizabeth. Braying

214

noisily, she **_charged_** out of the bathroom into the bedroom and galloped about, s c a t t e r i n g sand and seaweed.

'Not you again!' **shrieked** the receptionist.

Elizabeth **charged** out of the bedroom scattering the receptionist and the manager and Howard and Mr Bullerton and galloped up the corridor, snorting.

'SHOO! Naughty donkey, you!' said the receptionist, *chasing* after her.

'There's your culprit,' said the manager, to Mr Bullerton.

'Don't talk rubbish,' said Mr Bullerton. 'How do you explain the *"HOWARD"*?'

'I'm not so sure that's what it says after all, now I look at it again,' said the manager.

'Well of course not *now*,' spluttered Mr Bullerton, 'but—'

'If you'll excuse me, sir, I've got work to do,' said the manager,

217

setting off out of the bedroom and into the corridor. 'She's trouble, that donkey.'

'Correct,' said Leonard, CROSSLY. 'How am I supposed to get back to the beach now, mm? *Walk*, I suppose – bruises and all.'

Leonard set off out of the bathroom into the bedroom just as Mr Bullerton lunged at the manager, *slipped* on some seaweed, tripped over the

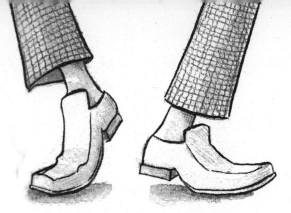

barrow and started to t^opp^le.

'WHOA!' **wailed** Mr

Bullerton.

'NOOO!' shrieked Leonard.

CRASH! went Mr

Bullerton on to Leonard.

SNAP! went Leonard's

claws on to Mr Bullerton's

bottom.

'WOO-WOOO-
HOO-HOO-
HOOOO!!!'
screeched Mr Bullerton, setting

off up the corridor at a quick

sprint, Leonard firmly attached.

'Is that trolley still outside?' said

Howard.

'Yes,' said Purvis. 'It is.'

'Then let's get out of here, fast,'

said Howard.

And they did.

HAVE YOU READ THE FIRST CRAZY Clumsies ADVENTURE?

If not then what are you waiting for? It wasn't Sunday Times children's book of the week and Telegraph children's book of the week for nothing, you know!

Howard picked up an empty water glass and placed it over the mouse. "You'll stay in there so I can eat my breakfast in peace. I shall deal with you afterwards…"

But you *can't* really deal with the Clumsies. From the moment when Howard Armitage first finds two talking mice under his desk, his life is turned completely upside down.

Obsessed with biscuits and forever hatching silly plans, the Clumsies are not your average mice – and they're only really good for one thing…

…*making a mess.*